THOMAS JEFFERSON
(1743–1826)

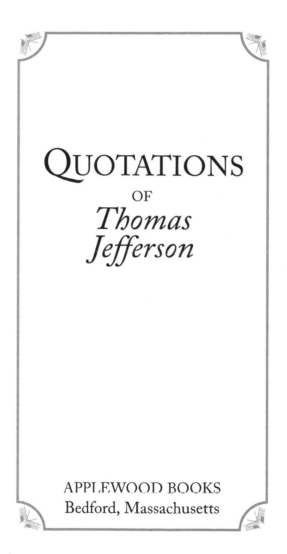

QUOTATIONS

OF

Thomas Jefferson

APPLEWOOD BOOKS
Bedford, Massachusetts

Thomas Jefferson

THOMAS JEFFERSON was born in Virginia in 1743.
He was born into a wealthy and socially promi-
nent family. Jefferson attended the College of
William and Mary, then studied law. In 1772, he
married Martha Wayles Skelton.

Although Jefferson was a writer of elegant
prose, he was not considered a very good public
speaker. As a member of both the Virginia House
of Burgesses and the Continental Congress,
he took on much of the writing. At the young
age of thirty-three, Jefferson drafted the
Declaration of Independence.

After the Revolutionary War, Jefferson was
appointed Secretary of State in President
Washington's Cabinet. He resigned in 1793 over
a disagreement with Alexander Hamilton. As
political disagreements continued to polarize the
young government, Jefferson found himself lead-
ing those who sympathized with the revolutionary cause in France. In 1800, Jefferson was
elected President in a tie vote that was decided,
ironically, by Alexander Hamilton.

After two terms as President, Jefferson went back to his home in Monticello, where he developed, among other projects, plans for the University of Virginia. Thomas Jefferson died on July 4, 1826.

QUOTATIONS
OF
Thomas
Jefferson

That government is best which governs the least, because its people discipline themselves.

Th: Jefferson

Information is the currency of democracy.

Th: Jefferson

A mind always employed is always happy. This is the true secret, the grand recipe, for felicity.

Th: Jefferson

No government can continue good, but under the control of the people.

*W*hen a man assumes a public trust, he should consider himself as public property.

*T*he boisterous sea of liberty is never without a wave.

*E*ncourage all your virtuous dispositions, and exercise them whenever an opportunity arises; being assured that they will gain strength by exercise, as a limb of the body does, and that exercise will make them habitual.

*D*o not bite at the bait of pleasure till you know there is no hook.

On matters of style, swim with the current, on matters of principle, stand like a rock.

Th. Jefferson

I served with General Washington in the Legislature of Virginia before the Revolution and, during it, with Dr. Franklin in Congress. I never heard either of them speak ten minutes at a time, nor to any but the main point which was to decide the question. They laid their shoulders to the great points, knowing that the little ones would follow of themselves.

Th. Jefferson

Honesty is the first chapter in the book of wisdom.

Th. Jefferson

Justice is the fundamental law of society.

One man with courage is a majority.

Th. Jefferson

Question with boldness even the existence of a God; because, if there is one, he must more approve of the homage of reason than that of blindfolded faith.

Th. Jefferson

I cannot live without books.

Th. Jefferson

A wise and frugal Government, which shall restrain men from injuring one another, shall leave them otherwise free to regulate their own pursuits of industry and improvement, and shall not take from the mouth of labor the bread it has earned. This is the sum of good government.

The bulk of mankind are schoolboys through life.

Th. Jefferson

Let common sense and common honesty have fair play, and they will soon set things to rights.

Th. Jefferson

I would rather be exposed to the inconveniences attending too much liberty than those attending too small a degree of it.

Th. Jefferson

The sovereign invigorator of the body is exercise, and of all the exercises walking is the best.

Books constitute capital. A library book lasts as long as a house, for hundreds of years. It is not, then, an article of mere consumption but fairly of capital, and often in the case of professional men, setting out in life, it is their only capital.

Delay is preferable to error.

Advertisements contain the only truths to be relied on in a newspaper.

Friendship is precious, not only in the shade, but in the sunshine of life; and thanks to a benevolent arrangement of things, the greater part of life is sunshine.

I'm a great believer in luck, and I find the
harder I work, the more I have of it.

Th Jefferson

*T*he care of human life and happiness,
and not their destruction, is the first and
only legitimate object of good government.

Th Jefferson

*S*peeches that are measured by the hour
will die with the hour.

Th Jefferson

*T*he most valuable of all talents is never
using two words when one will do.

*A*ll tyranny needs to gain a foothold is for people of good conscience to remain silent.

Th. Jefferson

*W*e are not afraid to follow truth wherever it may lead, nor to tolerate any error so long as reason is left free to combat it.

Th. Jefferson

*R*esistance to tyrants is obedience to God.

Th. Jefferson

*I*f people let government decide what foods they eat and what medicines they take, their bodies will soon be in as sorry a state as are the souls of those who live under tyranny.

*H*ealth is worth more than learning.

Th Jefferson

*A*ll, too, will bear in mind this sacred principle, that though the will of the majority is in all cases to prevail, that will to be rightful must be reasonable; that the minority possess their equal rights, which equal law must protect, and to violate would be oppression.

Th Jefferson

*G*reat innovations should not be forced on slender majorities.

Th Jefferson

*C*ommon sense is the foundation of all authorities, of the laws themselves, and of their construction.

*T*he legitimate powers of government extend to such acts only as are injurious to others. But it does me no injury for my neighbor to say there are twenty gods or no god. It neither picks my pocket, nor breaks my leg.

Th. Jefferson

I find the pain of a little censure, even when it is unfounded, is more acute than the pleasure of much praise.

Th. Jefferson

*T*he natural progress of things is for liberty to yield and government to gain ground.

Th. Jefferson

*A*lways take hold of things by the smooth handle.

I find as I grow older that I love those most whom I loved first.

Laws are made for men of ordinary understanding and should, therefore, be construed by the ordinary rules of common sense. Their meaning is not to be sought for in metaphysical subtleties which may make anything mean everything or nothing at pleasure.

Peace, commerce, and honest friendship with all nations—entangling alliances with none.

Never put off till tomorrow what you can do today.

Our liberty depends on the freedom of the press and that cannot be limited without being lost.

Th. Jefferson

The spirit of resistance to government is so valuable on certain occasions, that I wish it always to be kept alive. It will often be exercised when wrong, but better so than not to be exercised at all.

Th. Jefferson

An injured friend is the bitterest of foes.

Th. Jefferson

I am not among those who fear the people. They, and not the rich, are our dependence for continued freedom.

*N*o free man shall ever be debarred the use of arms.

Th. Jefferson

A nation ceases to be republican only when the will of the majority ceases to be the law.

Th. Jefferson

*T*he tree of liberty must be refreshed from time to time with the blood of patriots and tyrants. It is its natural manure.

Th. Jefferson

*D*etermine never to be idle. No person will have occasion to complain of the want of time who never loses any. It is wonderful how much may be done if we are always doing.

*E*very man is under the natural duty of contributing to the necessities of the society; and this is all the laws should enforce on him.

Th Jefferson

I hope our wisdom will grow with our power, and teach us, that the less we use our power the greater it will be.

Th Jefferson

*T*he beauty of the second amendment is that it will not be needed until they try to take it.

Th Jefferson

*W*here the press is free, and every man able to read, all is safe.

Whenever you are to do a thing, though it can never be known but to yourself, ask yourself how you would act were all the world looking at you, and act accordingly.

Th. Jefferson

To compel a man to furnish contributions of money for the propagation of opinions which he disbelieves and abhors is sinful and tyrannical.

Th. Jefferson

Nothing gives one person so much advantage over another as to remain always cool and unruffled under all circumstances.

Th. Jefferson

Every citizen should be a soldier. This was the case with the Greeks and Romans, and must be that of every free state.

*E*very difference of opinion is not a difference of principle.

Th. Jefferson

I am for freedom of religion, and against all maneuvers to bring about a legal ascendency of one sect over another.

Th. Jefferson

*N*o man will ever bring out of the Presidency the reputation which carries him into it. To myself, personally, it brings nothing but increasing drudgery and daily loss of friends.

Th. Jefferson

*T*he man who fears no truth has nothing to fear from lies.

Whenever the people are well informed, they can be trusted with their own government; that whenever things get so far wrong as to attract their notice, they may be relied on to set them to rights.

Th. Jefferson

When you reach the end of your rope, tie a knot in it and hang on.

Th. Jefferson

The will of the people is the only legitimate foundation of any government, and to protect its free expression should be our first object.

Th. Jefferson

I hold it, that a little rebellion, now and then, is a good thing, and as necessary in the political world as storms in the physical.

$\mathcal{D}$ifference of opinion is helpful in religion.

Th: Jefferson

$\mathcal{I}$ have never been able to conceive how any rational being could propose happiness to himself from the exercise of power over others.

Th: Jefferson

$\mathcal{S}$tate a moral case to a ploughman and a professor. The former will decide it as well, and often better than the latter, because he has not been led astray by artificial rules.

Th: Jefferson

$\mathcal{T}$he excellence of every government is its adaptation to the state of those to be governed by it.

*A*n association of men who will not quarrel with one another is a thing which has never yet existed, from the greatest confederacy of nations down to a town meeting or a vestry.

Th.Jefferson

*T*imid men prefer the calm of despotism to the tempestuous sea of liberty.

Th.Jefferson

*P*ride costs more than hunger, thirst and cold.

Th.Jefferson

*I*t is error alone which needs the support of government. Truth can stand by itself.

*E*nlighten the people generally, and tyranny and oppressions of body and mind will vanish like evil spirits at the dawn of day.

Th. Jefferson

*I*t is in our lives and not our words that our religion must be read.

Th. Jefferson

*N*othing can stop the man with the right mental attitude from achieving his goal; nothing on earth can help the man with the wrong mental attitude.

Th. Jefferson

*T*he greatest honor of a man is in doing good to his fellow men, not in destroying them.

$\mathcal{T}$he moral sense, or conscience, is as much a part of man as his leg or arm. It is given to all human beings in a stronger or weaker degree, as force of members is given them in a greater or less degree. It may be strengthened by exercise, as may any particular limb of the body.

Th. Jefferson

$\mathcal{V}$ictory and defeat are each of the same price.

Th. Jefferson

$\mathcal{T}$raveling makes a man wiser, but less happy.

Th. Jefferson

$\mathcal{W}$hen angry, count ten before you speak; if very angry, a hundred.

I like the dreams of the future better than the history of the past.

Th Jefferson

*T*he most sacred of the duties of a government is to do equal and impartial justice to all its citizens.

Th Jefferson

*L*eave no authority existing not responsible to the people.

Th Jefferson

*T*here is a natural aristocracy among men. The grounds of this are virtue and talents.

Whenever a man has cast a longing eye on offices, a rottenness begins in his conduct.

Th. Jefferson

My theory has always been, that if we are to dream, the flatteries of hope are as cheap, and pleasanter, than the gloom of despair.

Th. Jefferson

It is more dangerous that even a guilty person should be punished without the forms of law than that he should escape.

Th. Jefferson

Difficulties indeed sometimes arise; but common sense and honest intentions will generally steer through them.

*A*n enemy generally says and believes what he wishes.

*E*veryone must act according to the dictates of his own reason.

I believe that justice is instinct and innate; the moral sense is as much a part of our constitution as that of feeling, seeing or hearing.

*T*he happiest moments my heart knows are those in which it is pouring forth its affections to a few esteemed characters.

Walking is the best possible exercise. Habituate yourself to walk very far.

Th:Jefferson

Our greatest happiness does not depend on the condition of life in which chance has placed us, but is always the result of a good conscience, good health, occupation and freedom in all just pursuits.

Th:Jefferson

Never suppose, that in any possible situation, or under any circumstances, it is best for you to do a dishonorable thing, however slightly so it may appear to you.

Th:Jefferson

Happiness is not being pained in body or troubled in mind.

Governments are instituted among men, deriving their just powers from the consent of the governed.

Th: Jefferson

I can never fear that things will go far wrong where common sense has fair play.

Th: Jefferson

Independence can be trusted nowhere but with the people in mass. They are inherently independent of all but moral law.

Th: Jefferson

The liberty of speaking and writing guards our other liberties.

Th: Jefferson